Berna and Her Backpack

@2019 by Bernadette Amistoso-Morales

Published by Forerunner
Linden NJ, USA 07036

ISBN 978-1-64764-768-1

Printed in the United States of America

Cover design by Tina Wijesiri

TO GOD BE ALL THE GLORY

This is our family's story. In 2018, we experienced a devastating home fire. It was such a sad time for all of us. We lost everything except, (you guessed it right!), my backpack.

Our experience taught us that in a time of loss, we could hold on to our family, our friends and our faith to make it through.

This book is dedicated to our dearest Auntie Grace who opened her heart and her home to us. Her love and her generosity continue to carry us through in this season of many changes and surprises.

Most of all, this book is dedicated to every family and every child who has gone through loss or who is going through one. You are not alone. We are not alone.

Bernadette Amistoso-Morales

Berna and her family moved into their new home. "I am so excited," she said to her Mama and Papa as she looked at the beautiful park across. "Will you let me play outside with Sam and Chewey, Mama?" she asked. "Of course, Berna! After you finish your homework and chores, we will all go out and play."

Berna and her family filled their new home with joy and laughter. They loved eating her Mama's steamed rice and sweet chicken. Her Papa danced to his favorite music all the time. Her brother Sam and their dog Chewey played endlessly!

One early morning, Berna woke up to a strange and loud sound. It was the fire alarm! When she looked outside, there was smoke everywhere. Berna ran out of her room. She was so afraid.

"There is no more time! We all need to move fast," her Papa said frantically. As they made their way out, Berna grabbed her backpack. She wanted to save her things but it was too late.

In a few minutes, their entire house was burned down!

Berna and her family cried. There was nothing else they

could do. They prayed and comforted each other. They

lost everything - - - everything but Berna's backpack.

The days that followed were very sad. But thankfully,

family and friends gave them a place to stay. They also

gave them food to eat , clothes to wear and even toys to

play with. They prayed. They listened. They stayed close.

Time passed and Berna and her family found a new home. Slowly, they filled it with all the gifts and presents they received from family and friends.

Berna looked outside and loved everything she saw.
"O Mama, it's such a beautiful day! Will you
let me play outside with Sam and Chewey?"
"Of course, Berna! After you finish your
homework and chores, we
will all go out and play."

One night, Berna remembered the fire that destroyed her home. She also remembered everything her family had lost. She became very sad and began to cry. But later, she also remembered all the people who came to visit. She remembered everyone who gave, prayed, listened and stayed close. Berna began to smile. She wiped her tears away.

As Berna prepared to sleep that night, she reached out for her backpack and whispered to herself, " Tomorrow, Mama will cook steamed rice and sweet chicken. Papa will fill the house with his music. I will play outside with Sam and Chewey." She was super excited! She can't wait for the morning to come!

ABOUT THE AUTHOR

Bernadette Amistoso-Morales is an ordained minister, a writer and an educator. She and her husband Greg are blessed with two children, Caris Samuel and Rebecca Diane. The author was born and raised in the Philippines. She is the founder of Forerunner, an organization that leads seminars, retreats and provides various spiritual care services.

Mama's Sweet Chicken

3 lbs chicken, skin on and bone-in

1 cup vinegar or lemon juice

1/2 cup soy sauce

15 cloves crushed garlic

1 tbsp. ground pepper

1 tsp. salt

3 tbsp. sugar or honey

In a cooking pan, add the chicken, garlic, vinegar (or lemon juice) and soy sauce and bring it to a boil until the chicken looks cooked through. Add salt, pepper and sugar/honey (you can add or reduce to your taste.)   You can again sauté the chicken after it boils and add it to the sauce mixture, but even without doing it, the dish is ready to enjoy!

P.S. Mama's sweet chicken is perfect with steamed white rice! Yummy!!!

Made in the USA
Middletown, DE
31 January 2020